# BICYCLE
## *Madness*

Jane Kurtz

# BICYCLE

Madness

ILLUSTRATED BY BETH PECK

HENRY HOLT AND COMPANY

NEW YORK

*Henry Holt and Company, LLC*
Publishers since 1866
*115 West 18th Street*
*New York, New York 10011*
*www.henryholt.com*

*Library of Congress Cataloging-in-Publication Data*
*Kurtz, Jane.*
*Bicycle madness / Jane Kurtz; illustrations by Beth Peck.*
*p.      cm.*
*Summary: In the late nineteenth century, Lillie gains*
*friendship and help with a spelling bee from a neighbor,*
*Frances Willard, who braves criticism to speak about women's*
*rights and learn to ride a bicycle. Includes historical notes.*
*1. Willard, Frances, 1839–1898—Juvenile fiction.*
*[1. Willard, Frances, 1839–1898—Fiction.    2. Sex role—Fiction.*
*3. Bicycles and bicycling—Fiction.    4. Spelling bees—Fiction.*
*5. Friendship—Fiction.]    I. Peck, Beth, ill.    II. Title.*
PZ7.K9626Bi 2003        [Fic]—dc21              2002038881

ISBN 0-8050-6981-X / First Edition—2003
*Designed by Martha Rago*
*Printed in the United States of America on acid-free paper.* ∞
1    3    5    7    9    10    8    6    4    2

To my dad, who led a sit-down strike
for playground fairness when he was
in elementary school
—J. K.


For Laurel and Dominique
—B. P.

# BICYCLE
## Madness

*One*

*Hurrah, hurrah, for the merry wheel,*
*With tires of rubber and spokes of steel;*
*We seem to fly on the airy steeds*
*With eagle's flight in silence speed.*
          —*The Wheelman* magazine, June 1883

What an all-overish day this turned out to be at the
end of the strangest, saddest year of my life. I was day-
dreaming at my desk when I heard Miss Twombley
saying, "Boys and girls, I have a surprise for you." I
sneaked a look at my best friend, Minerva. Her eyes
were shiny excited. After a terrible two weeks—the
first weeks when we no longer got to see each other
after school every day—I think we were both ready
for something wonderful.

"In exactly one month," Miss Twombley went on, "we will have a marvelous spelling bee. Not only our class but all the students who are ten, eleven, and twelve years old will spell down in front of the entire school." Was it my imagination or did she look right at me? "You must be very well prepared to show what good little spellers you have become." Sometimes Miss Twombley had such a tight voice, it made me wonder if her shoes were squeezing her feet.

After we had all gone back to work, I looked again at Minerva. To pile on the agony—she was smiling a twitch of a smile. How *could* she smile at a time like this? I gave her the Face of Doom. Miss Twombley does not hold with any whispering in her classroom, but Minerva knew what I was thinking.

She rolled her eyes and made a little sign with her hand. I couldn't tell if she was trying to say that I shouldn't worry or if she was agreeing that I was doomed. Just in case she was trying to say that Miss Twombley was coming up behind me with a ruler, I looked down quickly.

I do so love it when words line up and march themselves into stories and other exciting things. But I hate the moment when it comes my turn to stand in

front of everyone and read out loud. And spelling out loud must be the most wretched pastime imaginable.

I scowled at the book that was open on my desk—*The American Spelling Book*. It had short lessons in it and lists of words we were learning to spell. Miss Twombley insisted on having a copy for each of us because she was determined to have a classroom full of excellent spellers. But I would be better off if Noah Webster, who wrote the book, had never been born.

My father is a good speller. My mother was a wonderful speller. But spellings spill from my mind like water. And when I stand up in a bee and try to spell the words out loud—*la!*—I could not be more miserable.

Last year, when our class had a spelling bee, I was the first person to shuffle down with my eyes on my toes. The very *first!* My face still feels hot and tingly when I remember what it was like to have all my classmates staring at me, whispering and secretly laughing. Now we would be in front of the entire school. I sat stiff and upright in my chair. No, I couldn't bear to have more embarrassment piled on all the other miserable things that had been happening to me.

"What are you going to do?" Minerva asked as soon as we were safely outside the door and the school day was over.

I remembered that twitch of a smile and I wasn't sure I wanted her to know just how skeery-like I felt. "In the yard next to my new house there's a buckeye tree," I said, as bold as anything. "I think I will be just fine if I hold a lucky buckeye every minute of the spelling bee."

She gave me a long and pitying look. "Oh, Lillie," she said. "I don't know if that's going to help."

I had to put my hands behind my back to keep from pinching her. I couldn't stand pity, having had quite enough of it since this time about a year ago, when my precious mother died. Luckily, I remembered the sentence I'd read only a few moments ago—"Never quarrel with your playmates." So I forbore, but my fingers itched as if spiders were dancing on them.

Minerva fluffed up her hair. "One of the older girls told me I look like a Gibson Girl today. Do *you* think I look like a Gibson Girl?"

I studied her. Had she figured out a new hairdo without me? "I think," I said, "that you look like a woolly mammoth."

Minerva gave me a terrible frown. I'm sure no Gibson Girl would ever be caught with a face looking like that! A few minutes later, she went gliding off with her arm hooked through Hattie's as if she didn't care one fig for me.

I did feel bad for telling her she looked like a woolly mammoth. But why does everything go right for Minerva and wrong for me? If I were Minerva, I would be walking toward my dear old home right now. And I wouldn't be worrying about a spelling bee, because letters would line themselves right up and dance calmly out of my mouth, even when I was standing in front of everyone.

I started home, staring at my toes. For my entire life, I had spent every afternoon playing and talking with Minerva. My mother, who loved lilies, used to grow tall white ones. Minerva and I would pull the yellow centers out of them, pick Mother's prize petunias, dress the yellow lily ladies in many ruffled layers of petunia dresses, and send them off to the ball.

Two weeks ago, without any warning, Father announced that our house made him too sad with its memories, and he had found us a new home on the other side of town. Almost before I could find my breath to speak, I was clopping off in the carriage, staring sadly back. That's when I realized that people were like helpless flies caught in a big sticky web.

Now I was a spelling *bee* caught in a big sticky web. Thinking about it that way made me giggle in spite of the thumping feeling in my stomach. It was just the kind of joke my mother would have loved.

I was almost home when I saw our new next-door neighbor, Miss Frances Willard, standing in front of her house. Oddly enough, she was holding on to a safety-bicycle!

I peeked at her. Should I run? Just yesterday, I was sneaking through the kitchen and heard Father tell Miss Plunkett, the housekeeper, that Miss Frances Willard was a dangerous woman. I asked my brother, Emery, about it, but all he said was that she gives speeches about menfolk forsaking saloons.

A carriage pulled up and another woman got out. Instead of fashionable big puffed sleeves, she wore what looked like a suit—not Father's fine suit with its silk hat and cutaway coat, but a long straight top over a gray skirt. Perhaps dangerous women had dangerous friends. A shiver slipped through me.

Miss Willard looked up and called to the woman. "You do know what this is, don't you?" Her trumpet voice was scary and firm.

I knew what it was. A safety. Those machines were all the rage now, but they never looked safe to me. They got their name because of being safer than grand old ordinaries with their huge front wheels. Emery said a man could go sailing over an ordinary's wheel and mash his nose all over his face. But safeties still looked wobbly. What did a woman like Miss Willard want with one?

She didn't wait for an answer. "This is a silent steed, swift and blithesome." She ran one hand along the top of the wheel. "Her name is Gladys."

I knew that "steed" meant "horse." But what was "blithesome"?

Was I in danger even if I just looked at her? I ducked behind an elm tree. "I never!" said the other woman. "Sometimes you take on the strangest ideas."

"You mustn't worry about me." For a minute, Miss

Willard looked like the biggest toad in the puddle. "It's not a velocipede or a grand old ordinary, after all. I've ridden a tricycle. I know I can learn to ride Gladys."

Ride her? Well, knock me over.

"What madness!" The friend gave her head an amused shake.

"Certainly not," Miss Willard said impatiently. "You sound like those people ten years ago who watched Miss Bertha von Hillern give exhibitions of her skill in riding a bicycle. They said she was a sort of semi-monster." She snorted. "Semi-monster, indeed."

"But you, my dear, are in your fifties." The woman wagged her finger. "Why take such risks?"

Even Miss Willard's reddish-gray hair seemed to bristle. "For three reasons. First, my love of adventure has been pushed underground too long and now it is bubbling up. Second, a bicycle is a powerful tool that will be under my foot." She gave her friend an almighty strong look. "Last, but not least, I shall do it because a good many people think I cannot at my age." And she laughed.

As soon as they had gone inside, I ran to my own house so fast you would have thought Gladys had turned into a real horse and was galloping at my heels. What an all-overish day it had turned out to be! My new neighbor riding a bicycle? Miss Frances Willard, like a brook bubbling up from under the ground? I wanted very much to see her do it. What a shame it was completely impossible.

# Two

*The little boy chuses some plaything that will make a noise, a hammer, a stick, or a whip. The little girl loves her doll and learns to dress it. She chuses a closet for her baby-house, where she sets her doll in a little chair, by the side of a table, furnished with tea-cups as big as a thimble.*

—*The American Spelling Book,* Webster

By evening, I was sitting in our parlor with a cold cloth on my forehead, having fallen into a fearsome fret. Mother always knew what to do with frets. She and Emery and I would write our problems down on paper and tear them into tiny pieces and scatter them from the top window. Should I try that? I sank lower in the chair. Without Mother it would never work right.

"Just don't think about that spelling bee," I told myself. A minute of pain and it would be over. But I knew that wasn't true. How many times had I remembered the class spelling bee and squirmed as if it had just happened yesterday?

Emery was reading his *American Boy's Handy Book*. I watched him for a while, kicking my foot against the leg of the chair. To take my mind from my misery, I finally asked if I could borrow the book to see how to make a boomerang.

Emery stared at me in surprise. "Why? No girl should have any reason to make a boomerang."

I sat up so fast that the cold cloth fell in my lap. "You oaf," I said. "You . . . you . . ." I was in such a splutter I couldn't think of what else to call him.

He got up, very calm. "Wipe the gum off your lip, Lillie," he said. Then out he went.

I'd heard the older boys at school say such things, but Father would never have stood for slang if he were here. I wished I had a boomerang to throw at the back of Emery's head.

Instead, I flung the cloth after him. I ran out of the parlor and up the stairs into Father's room. He wasn't home, of course. Since Mother died, Father had started working later and later. I opened the trunk in the corner very softly, so softly that even Miss Plunkett couldn't hear me with her sharp little ears. I buried my face in one of my mother's handkerchiefs. The smell of lavender made me want to cry. Carefully, I put it back and closed the trunk.

---

The next morning was Saturday. Now that I lived far from Minerva, I didn't know what I would do to make the long hours pass. At breakfast, Emery made a face at me. When I made one back, I wasn't fast enough. "Young lady," Miss Plunkett said, "your face will freeze in that position, and then what a fix you'll be in."

Father looked up from his *Chicago Tribune*. "Behave yourself, Lillie," he said, and went back to reading. I could feel Emery smirking at me while I finished eating.

After breakfast, I did my chores, feeling hot and wrathy. Finally, I dusted the last peacock feather on the whatnot in the parlor and could escape. Who should I see when I rushed out the door but Miss Willard and a young man with an elegant hat, standing in the yard admiring Gladys.

I crept to a hiding place behind my hedge. Father would worry if he knew what I was doing. For a moment, a lump of guilt stuck in my throat—but these days Father, who had always been kind and fun, never played the piano or sang his barbershop songs, never laughed and joked as he used to. Why should he care what I did?

"I will learn this bicycle exactly the way I studied the ABCs," Miss Willard was saying cheerfully. "I plan to practice for fifteen minutes every day, until I know the proper place of every screw and spring, spoke and tire, and every beam and bearing that make up Gladys."

I turned my head this way and that. If I squeezed my eyes just the right way, I could imagine I saw a horse there.

"Frances, I can't believe you intend to ride this thing," the young man said. "You know what all your friends are saying. You'll only break your bones and spoil your future."

Sadly, I had to agree. I could see the tips of Miss Willard's shoes under her skirt. What if the skirt got

tangled in the wheel? How many times had I heard Father's friends say that women couldn't handle the bridle and reins of a horse carriage? So how would they ever be able to handle the steering of a bicycle?

Miss Willard just calmly patted the front bars. "Many things have to be learned before Gladys and I can get on well together," she said. "But never fear. I will learn them."

I watched those two friends study Gladys. Seeing them smile and talk made me sorely miss Minerva. Suddenly, thinking about the way she trotted off with Hattie yesterday, I knew that things would never be the same again. And there was nothing I could do.

Before Miss Willard's fifteen minutes were up, I got tired of learning the place of every screw and spring and spoke and tire, so I ran down the block to find a tree that had caught my eye when I was exploring the week before. Yes indeed, there it was, and just the way I had remembered. Quickly, I looked around to make sure nobody was watching. I grabbed the lowest branch and pulled myself up, being careful not to show too much of my black stockings and ruffled drawers.

Suddenly, I heard Emery's voice coming from behind the fence just beyond the tree. This would be a perfect place for spying.

Sure enough, when I was high in the branches, I could see that Emery's friend Herman was drawing a circle in the dirt. Why did boys get to roam far and wide over the neighborhood when girls had to stay close to home? For a minute, I thought about spitting and seeing if I could get it to land in the circle. I had to press my lips together to keep from doing it.

"I've got a new shooter that's going to wake snakes," Emery boasted, holding up his new agate for everyone to admire.

I made a little hissing noise. These days Emery thought he was such a big bug. Before Mother died, Emery and I used to play games with her in our parlor every evening. Now he ignored me most of the time. When he did pay attention, he didn't care if he hurt my feelings.

"Bet you don't." That was Jacob. He passed his marble around. I could see Emery rubbing Jacob's marble, trying to feel if it was going to be better than his.

"Hope Jacob takes your new shooter," I whispered, but softly, so Emery couldn't hear me. I inched out along the branch, where I could see better. Just a bit farther now. Just a . . . Oops. The branch began slowly to dip downward. Oh, doom! I froze as hot fear gurgled in my throat. That was all I needed—to fall flat in a circle of marbles. Wouldn't *that* wake snakes!

# Three

[M]y feet are entangled in the skirt of my hateful new gown. I can never jump over a fence again, so long as I live.

—Frances Willard's journal

I eased myself backward, holding my breath. With all my will, I concentrated on thinking about marbles so I wouldn't imagine myself sprawling through the air, landing on my head.

Sometimes late at night, when I curled under my covers, wishing I could once again run to Mother's bed and rest my head against her while she whispered a bedtime prayer, I could hear the thump as Emery practiced marbles on his floor. And sometimes when Emery was outside, I crept into his room and held the cool, smooth marbles in my hands. The insides looked like magic worlds.

I reached the tree trunk and stuck there, peering through the branches. Herman and Emery put their marbles into the circle. Herman flicked his shooter. Clack. Right away, Emery's smoky went flying out of the circle, and Herman scooped it up. I was glad, even though I liked looking at the puff of color inside the glass. It served Emery right.

Jacob spoke up, putting his hands on his hips. "My pa says that Miss Frances Willard is going to break her neck. My pa says no female could control a cycle."

Before I could stop myself, I let out a surprised little moan. Luckily, a breeze was rustling the leaves. Otherwise, they would have heard me.

Herman gave his shooter another hard thumb push. One of Emery's mibs shot out of the circle. "*My pa says she'll get bicycle hands,*" he said.

Bicycle hands?

"And then," Herman went on in a low, dramatic voice, "she won't be able to hold a thing in either hand."

He sat back and looked around at the group. "My

pa says if women start riding bicycles they'll start wearing bloomers. My ma says—"

"We all know what your ma says," Emery interrupted. "She says the same thing my ma used to say and what everybody else's ma says."

The boys looked at each other. All together they said, "Bloomers! Well, I guess not!"

I considered dropping right down in the middle of their circle. "Who said Miss Willard was going to wear bloomers?" That's what I'd ask them. "She just wants to ride Gladys." That's what I'd say.

I knew I had to get out of there before I did something that would get me in trouble. I crawled and slid down the branches, as silent as a cat and just as fast. Oops! Too fast. I was almost at the bottom when my dress caught. I tried to stop. As I flung my arms around the tree, scraping my elbow, I heard a *riiiip*. Now I was more wrathy than ever at my brother, and Miss Plunkett was going to be enormously wrathy with me.

I walked home kicking stones and thinking of those boys saying, "Bloomers! Well, I guess not!" When I got to Miss Willard's yard, I stopped and looked around under her tree. Now I needed luck more than ever.

"I planted that tree with special seeds I brought from the East," a voice said.

I jumped, and my guilty heart gave a great thump. Miss Willard must have just stepped out onto her porch. "I only wanted one of the lucky buckeyes," I said quickly. Without planning to, I gave her a good, frank look.

Miss Willard looked right back. Her eyes had a fierce expression that frightened me. "You look very hot," she said calmly.

Did she mean my face or my temper? Though I did not want to get any closer, I was also afraid to go home. I glanced over at my house. Should I ask Father what to do?

I frowned. I wasn't a baby. What kind of danger was a respectable-looking lady who gave speeches all over? Trying to be as brave as any whale, I walked slowly to Miss Willard's porch.

She had a window box with bold red geraniums that Mother would have loved. How terrible could someone be who grew geraniums?

"On a day like this," Miss Willard said, "I wish I

were skipping barefoot after the plow with a pail of water, molasses, and ginger for the workers."

I leaned against the post at the bottom of the steps, a good distance away. Skipping barefoot would be fun. But there were no plows in Evanston, which was, after all, only twelve miles from the grand city of Chicago.

Miss Willard closed her eyes and put her fingers to her temple, as if she had a headache. I reached in back of me and tried to pull my dress out far enough so that I could see the tear. Maybe Miss Plunkett wouldn't notice. Just then, Miss Willard opened her eyes and looked at me in a knowing way from behind her nose glasses. Quickly, I let my dress fall back into place. "I try to be careful, but I always tear them," I said. "My friend Minerva never does."

Miss Willard sighed. "It would be lovely to be naturally good, wouldn't it? I had a young classmate like that. Her name was Effie. Once, I stepped on her toes at recess just to see if she would frown. She didn't."

A laugh burst out of me and I clapped my hand over my mouth. This was not a time for frivolity. "Our housekeeper is going to scold," I said mournfully.

"Ah." Miss Willard studied me with that strange, direct gaze. "But what will your mother say?"

"My mother is dead." I said the words right out and peeked at her to see if she would give me a look of wretched pity, as everyone else did.

She returned my look steadily. "So is my own dear mother." Her voice went soft. "She was the one who let me run with my brother and skip stones and make whistles with my jackknife."

A jackknife! Miss Willard's brother would have let *her* use a book that showed how to make a boomerang. "I wish I had a jackknife," I said. "Miss Plunkett says girls should only play with dolls."

She frowned. "Indeed! Well, I'll tell you a secret, but I have to speak softly, because if any dolls hear me they will roll their eyes, shake their heads, and whack at me with their wax hands."

I moved closer.

"I had a doll named Anna," she said. "One of my favorite playthings." She leaned forward, so I leaned, too. "Dolls are nice," she whispered. "But pets are far more frolicsome." She sat back. "So how did your dress tear?"

"I climbed a tree, Miss Willard."

She laughed. "I can see that you and I must be friends. Please call me Miss Frances."

I looked at her uncertainly.

She hurried on. "If we could only go to Wisconsin, I would show you the best tree in the world. I fastened a board to the old oak with the words THE EAGLE'S NEST—BEWARE. Neither my sister, Mary, nor my brother, Oliver, could come up."

I must have been staring at her in amazement, which is most rude, because she said, "Oh, it's true. I was not always the Miss Frances you see sitting here. Until my sixteenth birthday, I ran wild. Then came the long skirts and corset and high heels, and my hair was clubbed up with pins. I cried long and loud when I found I could never again race and range about."

Think of it! Miss Frances climbing trees. Miss Frances running wild. I wished she were my age now. I wouldn't care if Minerva never spoke to me again.

She sighed woefully. "My back hair was twisted up like a corkscrew and it made my head ache. I felt I should run away, but I hadn't the faintest idea where to run."

I thought I would burst with all this amazing information. What would Father think if he knew I was touching the porch of someone who had wanted to run away?

How odd. This new neighbor was not beautiful like a Gibson Girl and she was so much older than I was, but she was funny and fascinating, and her mother and mine had both died. Talking to her made me feel as happy as I had felt in the longest time.

Suddenly, though, a cold and skeery feeling swept me like a stormy wind. What would happen if Miss Frances really got bicycle hands and wasn't able to hold a jackknife or even a glass of lemonade?

"Now," she said in a voice full of longing, "perhaps I will have my beloved and breezy outdoors back. If I can learn to ride Gladys."

I hardly knew what to think. Should I warn her?

"Of course," she added in a fierce voice, "it's going to be difficult in these dresses women must wear that turn them into trussed turkeys."

I said good-bye politely and walked over to my own house feeling grum. Maybe the boys were right. Maybe Miss Frances really did want to wear bloomers.

Maybe, next time I saw her, her hands would be all crumpled up like thrown-away pieces of paper. It would be wise to stay away from her and Gladys. I had enough to think about just learning how to spell so I didn't make a fool of myself in the spelling bee.

# Four

[A woman] is a creature born to the beauty and freedom of Diana,
but she is swathed by her skirts, splintered by her stays, bandaged by
her tight waist, and pinioned by her sleeves until—alas, that I
should live to say it!—a trussed turkey or a spitted goose are her
most appropriate emblems.

—Frances Willard

I was at the porch before I remembered my own dress.
"How careless you are!" Miss Plunkett would hiss.
Maybe she would call Father in to scold me and tell
me one more time that the country was in a depres-
sion and this was not a time for new clothing.

I turned four slow circles trying to figure out what
to do next. Finally, I scrambled under the porch to pull
out my worn copy of *Little Women*, which I had stored

there for situations just like this. I had already spotted a special reading place for myself right behind the lilac bush.

When Mother became sick, I would sit by her bed almost every afternoon and read to her from *Little Women*. After she died, I turned to the part about poor sweet Beth over and over. Then I would wrap myself in one of Mother's blankets and cry.

Today I wanted to read about Jo. I was sure Jo would be Miss Frances's favorite March sister. And I was like Jo, too, wasn't I? Once, when Minerva was angry with me, she told me I was exactly like Amy.

Sternly, I made myself read the part where Amy was mean and selfish about the lemons. How could Minerva think I was anything like that? I was feeling indignant when I heard the squeaky sound of Father's buggy. So he hadn't even been home. A few minutes later, Father's footsteps thumped up the stairs.

I waited a little while longer before I eased out and put my book back in its hiding place. Perhaps Father would be sitting in his chair with his eyes closed, as he often did now when he came home from work. I could slither upstairs without anyone seeing me.

I had made it just inside the front door when I heard Miss Plunkett say "Miss Willard." I stopped with one foot in the air and my heart in my mouth.

"A bicycle?" Father's voice was full of astonishment.

I slowly put my foot down. Father had not told me I must never go near Miss Frances, but he did expect me to have common sense. If he mentioned that something was dangerous, he would probably think I should know better than to get close to it.

Miss Plunkett laughed a sharp laugh. "It *is* hard to believe," she said. "She must be fifty years old! I blame it on the changing fashions. Imagine my own mother trying to ride a bicycle while wearing her enormous crinoline. Why, a woman couldn't even stand too near the fireplace in one."

Mother once told me that her mother's crinoline caught on fire, and her friends couldn't get close. Luckily, she was smart enough to lie down on the hearth rug so they could wrap the rug around her and put out the fire. Otherwise, I wouldn't be here today.

At least Father and Miss Plunkett were too deep in conversation to be looking for me! I skittered toward the stairs. Father's voice stopped me. "The bicycle is simple foolishness," he said, "but other things about Miss Willard are plain dangerous. Fortunately, I understand she is often away from home, traveling around the country stirring up people, calling for votes for women! And let me tell you what I just heard. . . ."

His voice was rising. When Father was upset, it was a good time to skedaddle upstairs. I could imagine him clearly. His face would be getting red. His eyes, usually kind, would look sharp as steel traps, and his mustache would quiver.

Upstairs, I peeled out of my torn dress and tucked it behind my wing chair. I would find a better hiding place for it later. Meanwhile, I had a spelling bee to study for. I sat in the chair and stared at the ceiling, missing Minerva, wishing I could talk to Mother.

In the old days, Father never walked around looking worried and upset. He was a manager at the Zeno Manufacturing Company. Manager was a high and important position, just under the boss, but if he ever did come home in a grim mood, he and Mother would talk. Before long, I would hear him laughing.

Mother was that way. The day she told me about the dress that caught fire, she started to laugh so hard she could barely breathe. "I know it isn't really funny," she finally gasped, "but can't you just picture the women helping roll Grandmother and her big skirts up in a hearth rug?"

Father's friends called her sweet and charming, but she wasn't too timid to speak her mind. When I was a little girl, she shook her head over women's skirts with yards and yards of cloth in the back. "Look at all those pleats and flounces," she would say, as we sat together studying magazines. "Why, those women look as if they might be pulled over backward any minute." Last year, she complained about puffy sleeves that got in the way of everything. "I don't know how I would have survived wearing the full hoop skirts your grandmother wore when she was young," she would say to me. "And thank goodness we don't wear enormous bustles anymore. But these corsets! Wretched stiff things."

Last spring, Mother had just joined a Women's Club when she got influenza. Every time I went into her room, she was whiter and weaker, but I still never dreamed that she would leave us.

She would have liked Miss Frances—I know she would have. Except for Jo March in *Little Women*, I had never known of anyone so bold as our new neighbor, and Jo March only lived in a book. I leaped up from the chair, ran to the window, and looked down. It was more pleasant to try to see what was going to happen with Miss Frances and Gladys than to study my hopeless spelling.

# Five

*My sister and I stood at the window and looked out after [Father and Oliver]. Somehow, I felt a lump in my throat, and then I couldn't see their wagon any more, things got so blurred. I turned to Mary . . . and said, "Wouldn't you like to vote as well as Oliver? Don't you and I love the country just as well as he, and doesn't the country need our ballots?" Then she looked scared, but answered in a minute, "'Course we do, and course we ought,—but don't you go ahead and say so, for then we would be called strong minded."*

—Frances Willard

By the time I got to school that Monday, everyone was abuzz with the excitement of what was sitting on Miss Twombley's desk—a glorious fountain pen, the prize for the spelling bee. Each class would get to admire it for a few days, starting with our class.

I crept close to some girls who were standing and gazing at it and found myself beside Minerva. "With that pen," she whispered, "anyone could write splendidly. I think I could win it, don't you?"

I don't know what kind of fancy grabbed me. I longed to be friends with Minerva again. But I was in such a spite about the spelling bee that I heard myself saying, "I imagine you can spell down the older girls just because they've made you their pet now."

Minerva gave me a look of pure surprise and hurt. Then she walked off in a pucker. "You know spelling is one of my talents, and you just don't want to admit it," she said over her shoulder.

That afternoon, Miss Twombley gave us a lesson about the Great Chicago Fire. She showed us the Aleutian Islands on a map and said sailors who traveled to those far islands found that even people living there knew three English words—"Victoria," "dollar," and "Chicago." "As you can see," she said primly, "it's an ill wind indeed if it doesn't blow somebody some good. The roaring flames destroyed seventeen thousand buildings and left ninety-eight thousand people without homes. But the flames also touched the hearts of the world."

She talked about the fire as if we would surely remember it. Actually, it had happened more than ten years before I was born. Did people in the Aleutian Islands still talk about it? I was so full of my thoughts that I forgot Minerva and I weren't speaking. I looked at her, but she was whispering with Hattie. I hastily turned around again, my face burning.

All I could do then was slowly open my spelling book and try to study. "Bold, hold, fold, sold, gold." I stared at the list. "Gale, pale, sale, vale." If I didn't find some way to spell soon, Minerva and her new friends would have something crackerjack to laugh about.

---

After that morning, my stomach started to hurt every time I thought about school. All week, Minerva spent her time with Hattie or the other older girls. With their help, she somehow learned to fix her hair in an actual Gibson Girl pompadour crow's nest. I couldn't believe how much older it made her look. But I didn't care. After all, I had my own secret.

Miss Frances's friend Miss Luther was helping her with Gladys. Every day after school, I sat in a corner of the porch—where I couldn't be seen from the street—and watched them. If Father hadn't been so busy, he might have quickly discovered my hiding place, but he hardly ever looked for me. Emery spent all his time with his friends. Miss Plunkett was used to the way I found hiding places to read.

So no one knew I was learning about screws and springs, spokes and tires, beams and bearings. Miss Luther praised the pneumatic tires that would carry Miss Frances safely over pebbles. She pointed out that the gearing was safely tucked in, so a woman's skirts wouldn't tangle in it. But no matter what Miss Luther said, Miss Frances made no move to climb onto Gladys.

On Friday afternoon, Miss Luther said, "You know, Frances, it is only a bicycle after all. Maybe you should give up the idea."

"Oh no." Miss Frances had on her stubborn look. "Why, it's a freedom machine." She patted Gladys. "Susan B. Anthony herself believes these machines will do more to bring women the vote than anything else could."

The vote! Women had been marching around talking about voting since before Mother was born, but I'd many times heard Father's friends say it was folly and nonsense to think it would ever happen.

"Well . . ." Miss Luther gave Gladys a long look. "Let's start by just taking her for a stroll, then."

They walked down the sidewalk holding Gladys between them. I trotted behind, near enough to hear but not so close that people would think I was with them. "She's full of tricks and capers." Miss Frances was holding one crossbar. "Will I ever be able to hold her head steady and make her prance to suit me?"

Miss Luther was holding the other bar. "Don't forget what you always tell me about the woman question."

"We must creep before we can walk and then run." They said the words together. Miss Frances patted Gladys again and pushed her eyeglasses up on her nose. While they turned the bicycle around, I ducked behind a bush.

If they were talking about the vote, women had been creeping for a long time. People would never change their minds about that.

After Miss Frances and Miss Luther were halfway down the block again, I was about to move when I heard Emery's voice. "Can't play marbles," he was saying, "because you took all of mine. Just wait until I get another one. I'll win them back and more."

"Would you look at that," Jacob said.

For a moment there was silence. Herman was the first to speak. "My pa says women who ride bicycles will never have any children."

"I don't guess that's a problem for Miss Willard," Emery said.

"Also," Herman went on sternly, "she'll develop bicycle eyes. My pa is a doctor, you know."

Bicycle eyes?

"It happens because they have to hold their head down to ride," he explained, "but they keep raising their eyes to look ahead."

---

That night, I dreamed that I was standing in front of all the students in the school trying to remember how to spell "Mississippi." How many "s"s? One "p" or two? Half of the eyes on me were full of pity. The others were full of scorn. I woke up shivering.

After breakfast, I went to the tree in Miss Frances's yard and searched until I found the perfect buckeye. I bent over to pick it up. When I heard a creaking noise, I whirled around. Miss Frances was turning the corner of her house, leading Gladys all by herself. "Lillie, what are you doing under my tree?" she asked.

I held out the buckeye. "Do you believe in luck?"

Miss Frances paused to steady Gladys. "I believe in changing people's minds," she said firmly. "I always have. When my father decided it was too dangerous for me to join Oliver in riding the family horse, I put a saddle on Dime, our cow. The cow bucked, and I flew into the flower bed. But after that, Father let me ride the horse as much as I wanted."

How funny to think of Miss Frances flying over a cow's horns. "You really think women will be able to vote someday?" I asked.

"Yes, I do."

"But what if you're wrong?" I blurted. "What about all the speeches you gave for nothing?"

Instantly, I was embarrassed. But Miss Frances just said, "It *is* taking a long time. I can remember the very moment the seed-thought of voting was first planted in my young brain. My father came home to tell us about a great fight in the state of Maine to stop the sale of liquor. He couldn't bear the way some men took to drinking and completely forgot to care for their families. He said, 'I wonder if poor rum-cursed Wisconsin will ever get a law like that.'"

So her father thought that men should forsake saloons, too.

Miss Frances leaned Gladys carefully against the house. "My mother rocked a while in silence and then she gently said, 'Yes, Josiah, there'll be such a law all over the land someday, when women vote.'"

Didn't that prove it was hopeless? Miss Frances was old and her mother had died and still women were no closer to being able to vote.

Miss Frances sighed. "Even she dared say nothing more. In fact, many years passed before I heard anything else about such a dangerous thing. So tell me, why do you need luck?"

"Because of school," I burst out. "Father forced us to move here and now everything there is terrible."

Miss Frances nodded understandingly. "My father moved me to this neighborhood after my sister died and he couldn't bear the old house or anything in it. Come into Rest Cottage and I'll show you her picture."

I looked over at my house. Did I dare? I wondered if Miss Frances was angry with her father when he made them move.

"I think you'll be interested in the other members of my household," Miss Frances added.

That got my curiosity up. What kind of people would Miss Frances hide in her house? I walked carefully up the steps, ready to run if I had to.

The minute Miss Frances opened the door, I saw the kitten. Oh! I bent to pat it, and a large blue-eyed cat wandered up.

"I name my pets after those I've always loved," Miss Frances said. "The kitten is Mudge, after a kitten my brother and sister and I buried in our pet cemetery. The cat is Susan B. Anthony, after my friend who is very much alive."

Mudge and Susan B. Anthony were not the end of it. Miss Frances also had three birds that filled the parlor with sounds of chirping and skittering. Best was a big dog with patient brown eyes. "She came to live with me when my mother died," Miss Frances

said, "so I gave her my mother's nickname—Saint Courageous."

Saint Courageous was some pumpkins! Her head came up to my waist, and her feet were as big as boats. And Miss Frances had other wonderful things. Tiny pewter dishes she once played with. A sampler—the only needlework she ever finished, she said. A desk with ninety-nine compartments, one of them a secret.

Her study was full of pictures. I studied a painting of people marching, holding signs. Miss Frances showed me her mother and father, then pointed to the portrait of Mary. "My mother always said I was a comet but my sister was a beautiful shining star. Her death crushed out all my feelings for a while." She looked at me and our eyes met. I picked up a picture of Abraham Lincoln and studied it so I wouldn't cry.

Miss Frances cleared her throat. "When he was elected president, I shouted a great 'Hurrah!' Even if I wasn't allowed to vote for him, I'm sure I was as glad as any man who did."

That delighted me. Father said that Abraham Lincoln had the best and truest heart that ever beat.

Father! "I must go," I said. "Thank you for introducing me to the animals."

Miss Frances smiled. "They liked you. On Monday, I need to leave town to give a speech. Anna, my secretary, usually feeds my pets, but she's to go with me this time. Would you be willing to feed my animals and give Saint Courageous her walk, if I showed you how later this afternoon?"

"Oh, please, yes," I said. "I promise to take wonderfully good care of them."

Father wouldn't be happy, of course, but I had a good idea about that. If I explained to him how much Miss Frances loved President Lincoln, I just *knew* he would see that she wasn't a dangerous woman at all.

I walked home feeling determined. I'd bring home my speller every day and start studying. If Miss Frances could ride a cow, I could learn enough spelling words to keep from being totally and completely embarrassed.

# Six

*If you are poor, labor will procure you food and clothing—if you are rich, it will strengthen your body, invigorate the mind, and keep you from vice.*

—*The American Spelling Book,* Webster

I planned to talk to Father that afternoon, before Miss Frances showed me how to walk Saint Courageous, but when I went to find him, he was gone. "Why does Father have to work even on a Saturday?" I asked Emery.

"Because he's a manager, and the new Chief Factory Inspector is visiting him next week." Emery waved his hand toward the door. "Don't bother me. I'm trying to figure out how to get more marbles."

Because of the new Chief Factory Inspector, my Monday morning turned into a Great Chicago Fire disaster. Before I opened my eyes, all my responsibilities pressed down on me as if I were a load of clothes on the ironing board. I had an important job to do. And the spelling bee was only two and a half weeks away now. I felt as if I'd eaten a whole barrelful of pickles.

Then Miss Plunkett stepped into my room holding up the torn dress I thought I had carefully hidden. She was much too genteel to shout, but she did give her foot a stamp. "Lillie Applewood," she said. "Whatever am I going to do with you?"

I said I was sorry, sorry, sorry.

She kept shaking her head and scowling.

"Oh, Miss Plunkett, didn't you ever like to do things outdoors?" I thought about Miss Frances leaping over fences. Miss Plunkett pinned me with a sharp look and said that she used to go skating in a coat trimmed with fur and she never even once tore the blue poplin dress she wore underneath.

At last she left, and I thought the worst was surely behind me. But when I got downstairs, Father was pacing by the breakfast table staring at a paper in his hand and muttering. I had just put a spoonful of oatmeal in my mouth when Father suddenly looked up and said in a distracted way, "Emery tells me that you were walking with Miss Willard and a large dog on Saturday."

I shot Emery a baleful glance. As soon as I swallowed my mouthful of oatmeal, I would tell Father about Abraham Lincoln. But I never got the chance. "Perhaps I've been too busy to explain things properly to you," he said gently. "Please do not set foot on Miss Willard's property again. I wish your mother were here to explain, but she isn't, so you will simply have to trust me that it's your own good I have in mind."

The heat jumped into my face! "Wait . . ."

"Lillie." He looked down at his paper again. I had never seen him so huffed. "I'm too busy to discuss this any further right now. I will see you again this evening, and I expect I will not need to say anything more to you on this matter." He walked off, still staring at the paper. I half expected him to trip and fall flat.

I shuffled to school with my head lower than a worm's head, thinking my own thick thoughts. Susan B. Anthony and Mudge would probably survive, but I couldn't let Saint Courageous go without her food and walk. What was I going to do? I mustn't disobey my father. Now my stomach felt as if I had eaten a whole barrelful of crackers on top of my barrel of pickles.

———————※———————

What a grum school day! I longed to ask Minerva for advice, but she never looked my way. Miss Twombley rapped my fingers because I wasn't sitting correctly at penmanship. I sat by myself at lunchtime with only my lunch pail for company.

By the time I finally was home again, I could do nothing but curl in one of the parlor chairs in a ball of misery. I had adored our old parlor with its fans and umbrellas, whatnot and embroidered cushions, clocks, vases, china, and candlesticks—and the lovely pink conch shell that Mother would hold to my ear so I could hear the ocean. Best of all, I loved the piano, where Father would sit and play, coaxing Mother and Emery and me to sing along with him. This new parlor had all the same things in it, but it felt unfriendly and cold.

I thought about the way Mother's whole face used to turn into wonderful wrinkles of laughter when she found something funny. What kind of girl would she have been when she was my age? Nothing like me. In the trunk was a lovely suit of blue velvet trimmed with fur that Grandmother had made for her. "I felt so fine holding this fan of ivory and wearing this little cape, with my hair in a single braid cascading down my shoulders," Mother told me as she lifted each thing lovingly out of the trunk. "Your grandmother gave me my first pair of gloves at the same time, but they must have gotten lost."

I looked at the conch shell, wishing I could hear her voice in it instead of the ocean. What *was* I going to do? Saint Courageous must be whining and scratching the door by now, but Father had forbidden me to go there. I felt as if I had ropes on both arms and the ropes were being yanked in opposite directions. Suddenly, I heard the words "Miss Willard" in the kitchen. I crept behind the door and stood as still and straight as a knife.

"Not just *voting*," Miss Plunkett was saying. Her voice dropped, and all I could hear was "... the way things happened in Pennsylvania."

"What happened in Pennsylvania?" the delivery man asked.

"Oh, you must have heard." Miss Plunkett paused dramatically. "Workers at the Carnegie Steel plant shot some Pinkerton guards. Shot them! Then they began what they called a 'strike,' refusing to work. Factories all over this country are a bundle of tension right now, I can tell you! Many owners would rather go out of business than meet with workers to discuss complaints." She stopped and then burst out, "Why, Henry Clay Frick, the chairman of Carnegie Steel, was shot and stabbed."

Before I could stop myself, I leaped into the kitchen. "Miss Willard didn't stab him," I shouted. "She would never kill anyone."

Miss Plunkett was so startled she dropped the pie she was holding onto the floor. Her hands went to her neck and she gasped. "What a saucebox you've become ever since—"

She stopped.

"Poor motherless babe," the delivery man murmured.

"Mr. Frick didn't die," Miss Plunkett went on in a flustered voice. "Anyway, the strike happened last year. I was only saying Miss Willard gives speeches supporting worker rights. Now I'm sure you understand why your father calls her a dangerous woman."

After she shooed me from the kitchen, I stomped out to the front porch and opened my speller to the words not exceeding three syllables. "I-dle-ness will bring thee to pov-er-ty; but by in-dus-try and pru-dence thou shalt be fill-ed with bread." Yes, people had to work hard. The sampler over Father's bed said "Honor lies in honest toil." Factories were a place where even children were learning industry and pru-dence. I heard a friend of Father's say, "The factories need the children, and the children need the factories."

And getting shot—that was awful. Maybe Miss Frances was a beast, after all. But hadn't Father him-self told me always to keep my promises? On the other hand, what about "obey your parents"? Then again, if I obeyed Father, what about Saint Courageous? I almost imagined that I could hear her howling with hunger. I took out the buckeye and threw it as far as I could. Some luck! My head was a snarl, and there was nobody to help me out of my mess.

# Seven

*When [the bear] was fairly out of sight and hearing, the hero from the tree called out—Well, my friend, what said the bear? He seemed to whisper to you very closely. He did so, replied the other, and gave me this good piece of advice, never to associate with a wretch, who in the hour of danger will desert his friend.*

*—The American Spelling Book,* Webster

For at least half an hour, I rocked back and forth, hugging my speller. I was that little hopeless fly caught in a sticky web. Think. Think. There must be some answer. What would Jo in *Little Women* do? I shook my head. She would never disobey Marmie. What about Mother? She would never have gotten herself into such a predicament. What about Miss Frances?

Well, I knew what she would do. Miss Frances would run away from home.

At first, the thought just flickered past. Then I stopped and held on to it. I could get myself to Chicago by hiding in the back of someone's carriage. From wherever it stopped, I could walk to the railway station if I had to. When Uncle George came for Mother's funeral, he described all about the Pullman cars, with their soft seats, oil lamps, and dining cars serving quail on toast and plum pudding.

Uncle George told exciting stories of California and taught me how people talked there. And at the funeral he said he would have done anything for my mother. He gave me a gold coin to put in my savings. Why couldn't I use that to pay for the ticket? Uncle George said, "Why, a passenger could board the Overland Flyer in Chicago and step off in San Francisco three days and fourteen hours later."

Three days and fourteen hours was practically nothing.

Before I could change my mind, I hurried inside and up the stairs to Father's room. I needed something that must be in the trunk. Father couldn't have thrown it away.

I lifted the lid. There was the handkerchief with its lavender smell, the blue velvet suit, and the ivory fan. At the very bottom, I found it. I put everything else back and went downstairs, where I sat on the porch, staring at the house next door. Could I hear a faint barking?

Finally, I looked down at the picture in my hand. I could remember the exact day it had been taken. We were on a picnic, and Father pulled out his new Kodak camera, looking pleased and proud. At first Mother protested, laughing. That's when Father caught her in the photograph.

After she died, he never used the camera again. "He won't even miss me," I said to the picture. "He's never home anyway."

I stared at Mother. She used to let me brush her long brown hair when she unpinned it at night. In the picture, it was piled on top of her head. Her eyes were full of tenderness. In the months after Mother died, I was sure I had used up all my tears, but, sitting on the porch looking at the picture, I began to cry.

It was so miserable to have to leave home. What would Father and Emery think? What would Miss Frances say when she came home?

"Lillie?"

I gasped. Emery had sneaked up beside me. I was even going to miss him. I held out the picture without a word. He looked at it and then awkwardly patted my shoulder.

In that minute, he was so much like the old Emery that I told him about Father's forbidding me to go to Miss Frances's house, and how the pets were waiting. "I'm leaving home," I finished. "But first I have to go feed Saint Courageous. I just *have* to. Don't try to stop me."

I stood up and waited for him to say, "Wipe the gum off your lip, Lillie." He didn't, though. Instead, he said, "Father is only thinking about you. It might be dangerous to go into that house."

I jumped to my feet. "He just doesn't know Miss Frances. You two haven't been there. I have."

"But she wants women to be able to vote. Herman's father says that will make them crazy." He gave my hair a little tug. "I don't want you crazy."

Ooh. For a minute I thought I might give him a sockdolager to the nose. "*This* is making me crazy," I yelled.

Emery started to laugh. "Lillie, you're a real grit."

Hearing him say something kind took the fighting feelings out of me. "I don't feel like a grit," I said. Not with the thumb of doom about to come down on my head.

"Listen. You don't have to leave home."

He didn't understand. I opened my mouth to start all over again.

"I'll do it," he said.

I stared at him as if he had suddenly grown two heads.

"Father told you not to go to Miss Willard's house," he said. "He didn't tell *me*."

I didn't have to leave home? My brother was going to help get me out of the tangle? I suddenly loved everything—even this new house. Even Emery. Especially Emery. After I explained what to do, he made a funny, determined face at me. "All right. Here I go."

I ran upstairs and found a window where I could see all the way down the block. I watched and waited. Where was he? Shouldn't he be out by now? I couldn't stop tapping my fingers on the windowsill, so I made myself read the paragraphs I had copied from the speller.

*George, the sun has risen, and it is time for you to rise.
See the sun, how it shines; it dispels the darkness of
night, and makes all nature cheerful. Get up, Charles;
wash your hands, comb your hair, and get ready for
breakfast. What are we to have for breakfast? Bread
and milk. This is the best food for little boys.*

Where was he? Where was he?

Oh! There he was. And Saint Courageous was
walking on the leash, putting her big boat feet down as
nicely as you please.

*Moses, see the cat, how quiet she lies by the fire. Puss
catches mice. Did you ever see puss watching for mice?
How still and sly! She creeps along, fixing her eyes
steadily on the place where the mouse lies. As soon as
she gets near enough, she darts forward, and seizes
the little victim by the neck. Now the little mouse will
do no more mischief.*

I crumpled up the paper. I liked mice.

It was hard to know what to believe. I was sure
voting wasn't going to make women crazy. Miss
Frances's mother said women might vote for even

better things than men did. As for bread and milk, Mother thought oatmeal was healthier for boys. To tell the truth, I even wondered if working in factories could truly be good for children.

I stared down the street. All I absolutely knew for sure anymore was that if Emery and Saint Courageous could only get safely back to the house it would be a long time before I did any more mischief.

# Eight

*Let me tell you right here that these [jobs] involve work, hard work, deadening in its monotony, exhausting physically. We might even say of these children that they are condemned to work.*

—Lewis Hine, reformer

Emery was almost safely back to Miss Frances's house when it happened. Three houses down, I saw a man come out and close his front door. "No," I whispered. "No." It was someone that Father knew. *Run.* But it was too late. The man walked down the sidewalk and tipped his hat to Emery. I saw him turn and watch Emery walk up the Rest Cottage steps.

I'd have to tell Father right away—before the man did.

That night, I lay in bed thinking about how to do

it, my heart thumping so hard I thought the bed legs would start to rattle. Unfortunately, I fell asleep before Father got home, and the next day he was gone to work again before I got up in the morning. I could only hope it was too little time for that man to catch him, too.

After school, I paced up and down the yard practicing. "Father," I began . . . and stopped. What could I say next? I was so busy with my thoughts that I almost didn't notice Miss Frances and Gladys by the tree at the edge of our yard. "Good afternoon," Miss Frances said.

Father had said I must not go over to Miss Frances's house. He hadn't said I couldn't talk to her if she stopped by the yard and said hello. I glanced around. Tuesday was washing day, and Miss Plunkett was in the backyard hanging clothes on the line.

"Thank you for taking care of the animals," Miss Frances went on. "I brought you something." She held out her hand, smiling. The minute I felt my hand touch hers, I knew what she had. Marbles. Three of them. My favorite was the milky blue one. The second was small and clear green. The third had swirls of color in the middle.

I was opening my mouth to tell her what had happened yesterday when she said, "What a grand day this is. In just a few minutes, three young men with strong arms will be coming to my house to hold Gladys in place while I climb into her saddle for the very first time."

"Three young men?" How was she ever going to ride by herself if it took three of them just to help her get on?

Miss Frances mistook my surprise. "I do have men friends," she said. "Not like some of my women friends, who would not allow a male grasshopper to chirp on their lawn."

"Oh," I said. "No. I mean . . ." I stopped. "Miss Frances, are you ever scared when you get up to give one of your speeches?"

She shook her head. "In 1877, I spoke in Boston to five thousand people. People asked me, 'Aren't you frightened? Doesn't it make your heart beat faster to step out in that great amphitheater as the lone woman?' But I told them a woman who has taught the freshman class at Northwestern University can't be frightened of anything."

How I would love to stand in front of everyone and not be frightened.

Her eyes glinted behind her glasses. "Between you and me," she said, "as a girl, I was as fond of a romp, a joke, and a good time as any girl today—but when I became a teacher, I was determined not to let anyone get the best of me. My students came up with a plan to have one young man after another come in late. Each time someone opened and closed the door, a squeaky creak disturbed the whole class. That night, I took a lantern, a piece of soap, and a key and limbered up those hinges. You should have seen the look on the faces of the boys the next day when the door swung to and fro as if on velvet."

A carriage pulled up to Miss Frances's house, and I saw the young man who wore the elegant hat get out. "Splendid!" she said.

I crouched in my old hiding place behind the hedge. Another carriage pulled up with two more men and Miss Luther. First they discussed their plan. Mr. Elegant Hat took one of the crossbars. A man in a white hat took the other. That left the back for the man in the bowler hat.

"Don't worry," Miss Luther called. "They're all accomplished at riding the bicycle." She stepped into place with the camera.

Miss Frances lifted her long skirt just a bit and then carefully climbed onto her steed.

I clutched the marbles in my sweaty hand. Miss Frances was really going to do it!

"Ready?" Mr. Bowler Hat called.

"Ready," the others called.

"Forward, then."

She was moving! Wait. She was calling something. It sounded like "Woe is me."

"What did she say?" shouted Mr. Bowler Hat.

"She said *whoa!*"

"Whoa." They quickly stopped, and Miss Frances began to laugh so hard that they had to help her off.

She took a cautious step away from Gladys. "We all know the saying 'Fire is a good servant but a bad master.' I can see the same is true of my bicycle. But we will get along fine as soon as Gladys knows who is the master."

"And how will you show the bicycle that?" Mr. White Hat teased her.

"She'll do it!" Miss Luther said hotly. "You don't know what a hardy spirit Frances has. She's always beginning adventures. And she persists."

"Most of all," Miss Frances said, "I have patience to begin again whenever the last effort failed."

I wanted to pop up and say "Bravo! Bravo!" but of course I couldn't do that without giving myself away.

They helped Miss Frances climb on and off five more times. The last time, the funny little group walked a ways down the brick street and back. Then Miss Frances said that would be enough for the day and everyone must have some lemonade. As she went inside to get it, I could hear her muttering about women's tight shoes and dresses—"snug at the waist, chokingly tight at the throat."

I ran inside to get my own cold drink and study the way my marbles looked when they were under water. By the time I returned to my spot, Miss Frances and the others were talking about whether the Pullman workers would soon go on strike. "Don't you know that women in Chicago make twelve shirts for seventy-five cents and furnish their own thread and even finish off an elegant coat for four cents?" Miss Frances asked. "Children work twelve hours a day for a dollar a week. Greed for more and more money grinds workers into dust. I'm working on a leaflet about it right now."

"Aren't you afraid you're making a mistake, encouraging people to be lazy and take advantage of their employers?" Mr. Elegant Hat asked.

"The mistake," Miss Frances retorted, "is to treat the wage-earning class as a menace to the country when, in fact, they *are* the country. Have any of you had the chance to hear the journalist John Swinton?"

None of the other three had.

"How he works to help solve the problems of poor old humanity's bewilderment and heartache. He speaks as if words were being dynamited from his lips! They roar and ring, they scorch and hiss as he tells the crowd that women and children work for a crust as desperately as a drowning man works for a breath. He says, 'Anybody who can look at them and not cut his own throat is a scoundrel.'" Miss Frances chuckled. "Of course, I didn't remind him that *he* looked and never cut *his* throat."

What would it be like to stand tall and give a speech in words that rang and roared, scorched and hissed? For just a moment, I saw myself standing on the stage, the crowds cheering.

Miss Frances went on. "Men say to me, 'It is not because you women are inferior that we don't want you to vote but because you are too good and nice and pure to come into politics.' Well, we don't expect to leave political affairs as we find them. Not at all."

"Lillie." It was Miss Plunkett's voice calling out. I got up reluctantly. Twelve hours every day? Just one dollar for the whole week? Had the man who told my father that the factories were good for children ever heard John Swinton?

Before I ran off, I was relieved to hear Miss Frances say that she thought most labor disputes could be solved by talking—"or we shall be in for more times such as the Haymarket Riot. That wasn't a strike. That was practically a civil war."

By the time I gathered the sweet pinks that Miss Plunkett wanted for the table, Miss Frances and her friends were gone. I decided to go upstairs. Emery wasn't around, but I laid the milky blue marble on his pillow. Then I stood in the middle of my room, considering the pictures I had seen in Miss Frances's den. A plan was starting to bubble in my mind. I walked slowly downstairs and outside and began to pace the yard again, trying to work out my idea.

A bark startled me. Miss Frances was walking by my house with Saint Courageous. "Oh, I'm so glad to see you again," she said. "I started thinking I had perhaps left you with the impression that I am always fearless."

I thought about that. She wasn't fearless. I could see it was hard for her to ride the bicycle. But I couldn't imagine her feeling all shaky inside, the way I felt right now—and when I had to stand in front of everyone.

"Once, I climbed the tallest pyramid in Egypt," Miss Frances went on. "The wind began to blow fiercely as I reached the summit, until I could hear my panting breath and feel my cheeks becoming purple. Finally, as I crawled up to the topmost stone, the faraway voices of my friends faded, and I could hear nothing but the frightful sledgehammer beating of my heart."

"Miss Frances," I said impulsively, "when you showed me the picture of your father, you said what a great man he was. Did you ever disobey him?"

I could feel her eyes searching my face. "My father felt it was wrong to read novels," she said finally. "One day he took Mary and me to stay a month with some neighbors who lived six miles away. In their house I found the book *Jane Eyre*. When my father came to visit, he discovered me reading. You know, I never did finish that book."

Saint Courageous tugged impatiently at the leash. "Just a moment," Miss Frances told her firmly. "The very day I turned eighteen, though, I sat and calmly read *Ivanhoe* on the porch. Father came out. When he saw me, he asked, 'Have I not forbidden you to read novels?'"

I held my breath.

"'You forget what day it is, Father,' I said. 'I am of age—I am now to do what *I* think is right.' My father chose to see the funny side. He laughed heartily and said, 'A chip off of the old block.'"

I was so glad her father had seen the funny side. Would mine?

# Nine

*The chief wonder of my life is that I have dared to have so good a time.*
—Frances Willard

"Your father is certainly working late again," Miss Plunkett said as she helped me lay out my night-clothes.

Tonight I didn't care that he was late. More time to get ready. As I put on my long white nightgown and brushed out my hair, I thought about something I had heard Miss Frances say—that she believed in the eight-hour day for workers. Father could use an eight-hour day.

After I heard Miss Plunkett close the door to her own room, I pulled out the piece of paper, the bowl, and the broom that I'd stored underneath my bed.

I thought about one of the pictures from Miss Frances's den. The scene in the painting was in a big city— maybe Chicago. Hundreds of men were marching in a parade around a square. Some were carrying flags and drums. Others were carrying signs. "All men are born equal," one sign said. Another said, "Agitate, Educate, Organize." A third one said, "On to Victory."

I took out a pencil. I already knew what my sign would say. I made the letters big and dark. "I HAD TO DO WHAT WAS RIGHT."

In the bowl was the glue I had mixed up, using flour and water the way Mother did when I wanted to make cards with pictures from her magazines. I dipped my fingers in until they were sticky. Then I glued my sign to the broom handle and laid it carefully on the rug to dry.

Down the hall, I could hear the clink of the marble in Emery's room. He must be shooting it against something, practicing to get his marbles back. Finally, the clinking stopped. I picked up my sign and tiptoed past the paintings in the hall and halfway down the stairs. I settled myself on a step to wait.

At first, every creaky noise made me shiver in the dark. The bonging of the clock made me jump. A few weeks ago, I would have said I couldn't do this. Now I had met Miss Frances.

After a while, I got so sleepy that I had to lean my head against the wall and close my eyes.

*Whomp!* The next sound I heard was someone tripping over the small table that stood by the stairs. My eyelids popped open. The house was so dark. I made myself into a tiny ball. Then I smelled sulfur and saw Father's face lit by the glow of the small oil lamp in his hand. "Lillie?" he said. "What are you doing?"

I took a deep breath. Miss Frances had climbed to the top of a huge pyramid. Just today, she had tried to ride a bicycle even though she was scared. "I'm on strike," I said. I tried to make my words scorch and hiss, but they just squeaked.

My father didn't say anything. I thought my thumping heart would wake the whole house. He walked slowly up each step until he got to where I was sitting. Then he sat down on the stair beside me. "What do you know about strikes?"

"I know what the newspapers are saying," I said stubbornly. "Put men to work and let babies go home!"

My father gave a tremendous sigh. "I was afraid I might be one of those men. They are walking the streets of Chicago by the hundreds trying to find jobs. But the Chief Factory Inspector came today, and she wasn't the monster some had made her out to be."

The inspector was a woman? I wondered if she and Miss Frances knew each other. As I thought about Father's words, my stubbornness melted away. I guess he was angry with me because he was worried about his job.

"Mrs. Kelley, the inspector, told me of girls just your age in some factories sitting hour after hour at giant, noisy machines and being kept awake by having cold water thrown in their faces."

I shook my head, trying to imagine feeling as tired as I was right now and not being able to sleep.

He lifted me into his arms and walked back downstairs. Once we were in the parlor, he sat in the rocking chair. "All right," he said. "Let me hear what you have to say."

It all came flooding out—about the spelling bee and how Minerva and I weren't friends anymore. About how hard it was to live in a new house and not next door to Minerva. About how much I missed Mother. About Saint Courageous and what Emery and I had done. "You always taught me that I must work

hard and be responsible," I said. "And I was responsible for the dog. Besides, Miss Frances isn't dangerous. She would have voted for Abraham Lincoln."

I could feel him stiffen. Before he could squeeze out a word, I said, "I just know Mother would understand."

Father relaxed. After a few minutes, he said, "Is Miss Willard a good friend to my poor motherless daughter, then?"

Quickly, while I had a chance, I told him about Miss Frances—about how she grew up in Wisconsin, where she could romp and never saw the inside of a schoolhouse when she was a girl, but how she became a teacher anyway. How she just wanted things to be fair. "She can help me with my spelling," I said. "I know she can."

"I've been working long hours," Father said sadly. "You must believe me that I'm doing it for you and Emery."

I didn't say that I also knew how his work kept the mournfulness away so he wouldn't have to think about Mother.

"For so long I wondered if Mrs. Kelley, the first factory inspector, truly might be monstrous," he went on. "And just at this important time—a mere month after Zeno Manufacturing Company began to produce a new flavor of gum for Bill Wrigley to sell. We're competing with two other companies by calling our flavor Juicy Fruit."

We rocked for a few minutes in quiet. I timidly put my hand up to Father's neck and felt his heart beating. Then he said, "I don't feel right about letting you go into that woman's house. But if you want to talk with Miss Willard and let her share some of the things that your mother would show you if she were still alive—that I can accept."

I let him carry me up to bed and tuck me in, just like a baby.

---

The next two weeks were wonderful. Every day, after school, Miss Frances and Gladys and I went for a walk. Miss Frances told me stories about Jack and his beanstalk, and Blue Beard. We read *Little Women* to each other. We sat on my porch and she showed me pictures of wolves and sand-hill cranes and told me all about her pets, including Stumpy, a chicken whose legs froze off but who knew so much that it could almost talk. We played marbles. She told me about how her mother defended her when one of Oliver's friends said, "You're only a girl. You can't play with us," and how her father would ask, "Have you got the victory in you?" I began to feel as if I knew Oliver and Mary, her parents, and her witty old grandmother.

Some days, Miss Frances did what Father might have called dangerous things—she showed me a magazine article by a man named Jacob Riis, writing about the hungry children of New York, who had to breathe air fouler than the mud of the gutters. She said, "I believe my mother was born to be a senator and never got there." Some days, she told me about her travels to other countries. "Those far-off lands often made me very sad," she said. "I hadn't known what a wide world it is and how full of misery."

Most of all, every day we studied spelling. Miss Frances started me with the words of one syllable and then went to the easy words of two syllables accented on the first, and then the easy words of two syllables accented on the second. She showed me how to find little words within the longer ones. For words that kept tripping me, she made up interesting ways to remember the order of the letters or told me the stories behind the words. "Actually," she said, "you are a good speller. I believe it comes from your reading. You've only let your fear of reading aloud get in your way." Listening to her, I was sure I could last to the middle of the spelling bee and not be the first one down.

On Saturday, Miss Luther and another young woman showed up at Miss Frances's house. With Miss Frances sitting on the saddle, the two women pushed with all of their power until they were red in the face, each on one crossbar, so that Miss Frances could stay upright. Miss Frances pedaled while they trotted beside, steadying Gladys as well as they could.

That Sunday, Father was full of smiles. The salesmen were saying Juicy Fruit gum would be a big success. Almost all the shopkeepers in Chicago had agreed to put it on their shelves. Now his company was working on a new flavor called Spearmint.

After church, he pulled Emery and me to the piano and we sang loud and long, every song we could think of, including the popular "Daisy Bell." Emery and I harmonized on the last part, "a bicycle built for two." I laughed to hear our voices together and to think of Miss Frances on her bicycle.

Every day that next week, I found a stick of Juicy Fruit gum in my lunch pail. By the time Saturday came, I was in a fine mood. Miss Frances and I worked on the words of three syllables . . . "arrival," "amazement," "decipher," "decorum."

"Can I do it?" I asked. "The spelling bee will be here next Friday."

"Do it?" She gave me a firm look. "As my mother would tell me, of course you'll do it. What else could you do?"

"Amazement," I said. "A-M-A-Z-E-M-E-N-T."

She laughed. "You've got the victory in you now. I'm having the most royal time."

With her, I always had the most royal time, too.

In the afternoon, we put up the book. I was awiggle with excitement. It was finally time for Miss Frances to ride the bicycle. Now Miss Luther did not hold on to the crossbar at all but stood in back of Gladys. Three other friends stood nearby.

"I'm not sure," Miss Frances said. She looked at all of us, her friends gathered around, and took a deep breath.

"You've got the victory in you, too," I said.

She laughed. "So I have."

In spite of my brave words, I didn't want to look. What if she fell over and mashed her nose? What if she suddenly got bicycle hands or eyes? What if . . .

Miss Luther put her hand on the seat. "I shall be right here."

Could Miss Frances do it? Would she?

Slowly, Miss Frances began to pedal.

"Go!" I shouted. "Go, Gladys, go!"

Miss Luther ran behind, steadying Gladys. But Miss Frances began to go faster and faster, and finally Miss Luther had to let go. Off Miss Frances went, with all of us shrieking and laughing our encouragement. We couldn't have been more pleased if Miss Frances had suddenly grown wings and gone flapping into the air.

Emery, Jacob, and Herman came running from their marbles game. Miss Plunkett ran out onto the porch. I could see heads pop out of windows all along the street.

"Hooray!" I shouted, not caring who could hear me. "You're doing it, Miss Frances! You're really doing it!"

That evening, as we walked Saint Courageous, Miss Frances told me that her legs were trembling. "I will have to get stronger by riding fifteen minutes every day," she said. "Today Gladys spoke to me. She said she didn't ask me to climb on her, but now that I did, I must remember two rules."

We had to wait for Saint Courageous to stop barking at a squirrel. "The first rule she said was: 'Make up your mind quickly or I will toss you into yonder puddle and no blame to me and no thanks to yourself.'"

I laughed, and Saint Courageous turned her panting head to look, as though she were laughing, too.

"Second, she said I must not look down like an imbecile at the front wheel but must look up and out."

"Up and out," I repeated. It was the way Miss Frances had always lived. Up and out.

## Ten

*Daisy, Daisy, give me your answer, do.*
*I'm half crazy all for the love of you.*
*It won't be a stylish marriage.*
*I can't afford a carriage.*
*But you'll look sweet, upon the seat*
*Of a bicycle built for two.*
　　　　—"Daisy Bell," song by Harry Dacre, 1892

On Monday, when I got to school, everyone was buzzing about how it was only five days to the spelling bee. Who would win the fountain pen? By now, I had studied so many words with Miss Frances that I probably muttered them in my sleep. No matter what anybody else thought, I knew I had a chance.

When it was my turn to read aloud, I stood up and read my sentences firmly: "Play no tricks on them that sit next to you; for if you do, good children will shun you as they would a dog that they knew would bite them. He that hurts you at the same time that he calls you his friend, is worse than a snake in the grass."

"Very good, Lillie." Miss Twombley's voice sounded surprised. I sneaked a look at Minerva. Wouldn't she be astonished when the spelling bee came and she found out all the things I had learned!

The glow stayed with me through math. It stayed with me through our science lesson on birds. "Fowls which delight chiefly to fly in the air, and light and build nests on the trees," we read, "have their toes divided, by which they cling to the branches and twigs. The vulture and the hawk, which feed on flesh, have strong claws, to catch and hold small animals, and a hooked bill to tear the flesh in pieces."

The glow was still with me at lunchtime. And that's when I made my mistake. The older girls were standing in a group, talking. Hattie was there, of course. And Minerva was hanging on the edge with her mouth open, eagerly listening to everything they had to say. Without meaning to, I found myself creeping closer.

"Mrs. Astor's ballroom in New York holds four hundred people," a girl named Mildred was saying. "They say her dances cost thousands of dollars and she gives champagne and diamond tiaras to everyone."

All the girls fluttered their hands in front of their faces as though they were holding fans.

I made a face.

"I heard of one of the New York dinners," Hattie said, "where hundreds of white doves went flapping among the guests."

"And I heard of one," Mildred added, "where each lady found a gold bracelet when she unrolled her napkin."

"La!" Minerva put both hands to her cheeks.

Hattie sighed. "Wouldn't you just love to be a millionaire? According to my mother, Mrs. Stuyvesant Fish gave one dinner for her pet monkey and dressed it up in formal clothes as the guest of honor. My dream is to go to a party like that someday." Minerva nodded as if she were ready to run out and scoop that little monkey right into her arms.

"A few streets away," I blurted out, "forty families are packed into five old houses that were supposed to hold one family each." I couldn't believe I was saying this. "What about a three-year-old child in New York who makes five hundred artificial flowers and only gets paid five cents?"

Hattie whirled around. "Oh," she said. "It's you. Where's your bicycle?"

All the other girls started to laugh. What a muff I was. Why hadn't I kept my mouth shut?

Hattie stared at me with vulture eyes. And I, I suddenly knew, was just a little bird with divided toes, clinging to a twig.

Hattie began to sing.

> *"Lillie, Lillie, give us your answer, do.*
> *Is Miss Willard crazy? And for that matter, are you?"*

Now other girls were running over to listen. I opened my mouth and shut it again. I could feel all their staring eyes on me. Hattie sang on:

> *"No wonder she never got married.*
> *She refuses to ride in a carriage.*

*But won't it look silly,*
*Miss Willard and Lillie*
*On a bicycle built for two."*

Everyone knew the tune, of course. Hattie started over and the others began to join in. I turned and ran inside the school. But I could still hear their voices floating up through the open windows. I spluttered. I shook. Then I took hold of myself. Enough hissing and moaning.

Just wait for the spelling bee. I would stand on the stage looking triumphantly down at their faces while they were the ones to have to sit primly with their hands in their laps—Hattie and the other older girls. Minerva most of all.

All afternoon, I looked out the window. And when the last bell of the day rang, I rushed out of the school doors so fast my legs almost buckled.

"Lillie?"

I turned. It was Minerva.

"What Hattie did was awful." Her eyes were full of pity.

"Don't worry about me," I said fiercely. "I can take care of myself."

I ran all the way home. Miss Frances was in her yard, studying Gladys. I didn't want to embarrass her by repeating the song, but my words about Minerva's hatefulness came rushing out.

Miss Frances leaned over to look at Gladys's wheel. When she straightened up, she told me about a time when her father had bought her a red hood. "I hated it with a hatred and a half, but all the same I had to wear it." She took her hat off. "You can imagine how the red hood looked with my red hair."

Miss Frances put her feet carefully on either side of Gladys, holding the crossbars steady. "One girl in particular teased me unmercifully. Finally, I stood up to her."

"What happened?" Why was Miss Frances always so much braver than I was? I wished I hadn't run away.

Miss Frances laughed. "Oh, that girl became one of my best friends. I had a hot temper, but it was a swift electric flash. It was over very quickly." She put one foot on the pedal, waved, and rode off down the block.

I shook my head, still feeling cross as a pig in a bucket. I would never get over my feelings about Hattie and that song. But I would have revenge. One by one, I would see them sit down, with all the other students staring. And I? I would be standing tall, correctly spelling one word after another. For once, people would be staring at me, not with pitying eyes, not with mocking eyes, but with admiration and awe.

*Eleven*

*Freddie, Freddie, here is my answer true.*
*I'm not crazy all for the love of you.*
*If it won't be a stylish carriage,*
*I guess there will be no marriage.*
*For I'll be switched, if I'll be hitched*
*On a bicycle built for two.*

—Popular parody, author unknown

The night before the spelling bee, I got up and stared out the window at the tree branches waving against the moon. I imagined that they were waving, cheering for me. Miss Frances and I had gone all the way to the end of the speller, all the way to the irregular words like "busy" and "colonel" and "beaux." Even if I had three more weeks, I wouldn't be any more ready.

At the end of the bed, I touched my little packet. I had gotten Mother's ivory fan out of the trunk, and I was going to take my marbles—not for *luck* but so I would think of Mother and Miss Frances if fear grabbed hold of me. I put the fan to my cheek, feeling its cool smoothness. Then I got back in bed and closed my eyes, trying to relax.

Spelling words danced in my brain like fleas. How many times had I looked at those lists? How many times had Miss Frances and I practiced every word? I swallowed. In a way, I wished I hadn't read to the last page, because the book ended with something called a "moral catechism."

> *By what rule should anger be governed?*
> *We should never be angry without cause. It is wrong, it is mean, it is the mark of a little mind, to take fire at every little trifling dispute.*

I frowned in the darkness. All the things Minerva had done were more than trifling disputes. But the next part of the moral lesson made me squirm.

*What is revenge?*
*It is to injure a man because he has injured us.*
*Is this justifiable?*
*Never, in any possible case. 'Tis nobler to forgive.*

No matter what old Noah Webster thought, I was going to be happy for my revenge. I wished Father could be there, but he would be busy making Juicy Fruit. Miss Frances was off giving a speech. Emery would at least see my triumph. The thirteen-year-olds were too old for the spelling bee, but they were getting out of class to be able to watch and cheer.

---

It was one thing to imagine tree branches waving, and something completely different to stand on the stage the next day and look out at a forest of faces. For a long minute, my stomach tied itself into that old familiar knot of terror. I touched the fan that I was holding in my lap. "Help me, Mother," I whispered. I swallowed hard, glad that I wasn't going to be the first one to spell. I'd probably only be able to give a weak croak.

I clung to the edge of my hard chair and made myself picture Miss Frances instead of all those eyes staring at me. I pretended I *was* Miss Frances. Standing tall in front of my class while the door opened with a loud, squeaky creak. Holding my head up in front of five thousand people in spite of the whispering.

Each of us stood when it was our turn, walked to the edge, and heard the judge read our word. We all knew the rules. We must say the word, spell it, say it again, and listen for the weighty judgment: "That is correct" or "That is not correct."

At first, the words were from the easiest lists, and not even the ten-year-olds went down.

"Blank. B-L-A-N-K. Blank."

"That is correct."

"Chide. C-H-I-D-E. Chide."

"That is correct."

Then came the first stumble.

"Fuel," said a boy in a class below mine. "F-U-L-E. Fuel."

"That is not correct."

I heard the whispers. Near the back, someone smothered a giggle. It could have been me shuffling down. I was so glad it wasn't.

The words began to blur together. I stood up, spelled words, sat down. Stood up, spelled words, sat down. All around me, people were walking off the stage. But my mind was clear and strong as the words got harder and harder. Not one word came up that Miss Frances and I hadn't studied. "Promise. P-R-O-M-I-S-E. Promise."

"That is correct."

"Wrangle. W-R-A-N-G-L-E. Wrangle."

"That is correct."

"Zephyr. Z-E-P-H-Y-R. Zephyr."

"That is correct."

Hattie stood up. "Malign," the judge read.

"Malign," she said confidently. "M-A-L-I-N-E. Malign."

"That is not correct."

It was Hattie's turn to shuffle down with her eyes on her toes. I didn't dare gloat yet. I still had others and Minerva to beat. "Up and out," I whispered, rubbing my fingers against the marbles and the fan. "Up and out." I looked at the audience. My eyes caught Emery's, and he winked. I looked down quickly so I wouldn't lose my concentration.

"Profession. P-R-O-F-E-S-S-I-O-N. Profession."

"That is correct."

"Erosion. E-R-O-S-I-O-N. Erosion."

"That is correct."

Suddenly, when I turned away from spelling what felt like my hundredth word, I was startled to realize that there were only two people left on the stage.

One of them was me. The other was Minerva. I didn't look at her. All I had to do was keep on spelling those words.

Ferocity. My word. "F-E-R-O-C-I-T-Y. Ferocity."

"That is correct."

Original. Minerva's word. "O-R-I-G-I-N-A-L. Original."

"That is correct."

On and on we went. Could there be many more words left in Noah Webster's speller? While I was sitting, I glanced at Emery leaning forward in his seat, cheering me on.

I had forgotten what an excellent speller Minerva was. But by now I had gotten to be an excellent speller, too. I glanced at her as I walked back to my seat and she stepped forward. I could win. I just knew I could. *Snake in the grass.*

"Decipher," the judge said to Minerva.

"Decipher. D-E-C-I-P-H-E-R. Decipher."

"That is correct."

I stood up. She had just gotten a hard one—one of the hardest. I felt a flash of admiration. Why was it, exactly, that Minerva and I had stopped being friends? "Lillie," the judge said. I walked forward.

"Belligerent," said the judge.

Belligerent. That was Minerva and me. But who had started being belligerent? I swallowed. How did the word end? With an "-ant" or an "-ent"? I was like Miss Frances at the top of the pyramid, feeling the frightful sledgehammer beating of my heart.

"Belligerent," I said. I rubbed the marble once for good luck. "B-E-L-L-I-G-E-R-A-N-T." I didn't even pause. "Belligerent."

Neither did the judge. "That is not correct," he said calmly. "Minerva?"

Minerva stood up and stepped forward. I felt my legs shaking.

"Belligerent," she said. Her eyes were shining as they did when we made flower dolls in my mother's garden and laughed ourselves silly taking our dolls to the ball. Don't get it right, I thought. Please don't.

"B-E-L-L-I-G-E-R-E-N-T. Belligerent."

It was over.

In my throat, my breath fluttered like bats' wings. Off the stage, I could see Miss Twombley stepping forward with the fountain pen in her hand. I could hear people starting to cheer. Minerva turned to me and opened her mouth. I stood frozen, waiting to hear what she was going to say.

# Twelve

*I began to feel that myself plus the bicycle equaled myself plus the world, upon whose spinning wheel we must all learn to ride, or fall into oblivion and despair.*

—Frances Willard

"Man alive!" Minerva said. "You've become an excellent speller."

We stared at each other, and neither one of us blinked. All at once I knew. I had been belligerent. I was the snake in the grass, not Minerva. The embarrassing truth was that I'd wanted to be angry with Minerva because of everything that was happening to me, but the hard things weren't her fault. She wasn't to blame for my mother's death or the move or the spelling bee—or even for the teasing in the schoolyard.

What would Miss Frances do? What would Mother do? I knew, of course. "I'm glad you won the fountain pen," I said. "Your writing will be beautiful."

"Oh, Lillie," she said. "Thank you. You did such a good job."

Out of the corner of my eye, I saw Miss Twombley stepping onto the stage, holding the beautiful fountain pen. "I've been studying with Miss Willard," I said. "After school."

Minerva didn't even glance at the pen. "Couldn't we find some way to see each other after school again?" she asked. "And what about summer vacation? I miss doing things with you."

I smiled. I had a perfect idea. When Minerva leaned close I whispered, "I'm going to ask my father if he can afford to buy me a bicycle."

Minerva smiled. It hardly stung at all for me to step back and watch Miss Twombley hand her the pen.

I skipped home, thinking about my new plans. After the spelling bee, so many people had come up to me to say I had been amazing. Even Miss Twombley had said, "Lillie, you are full of surprises." I could hardly wait to tell Miss Frances about everything.

When I got to my house, Miss Frances was sitting on her porch. Gladys was lying on her side in the yard. I had never seen the bicycle flopped over like that before.

"Miss Frances, what's wrong?" I asked, running up. "What's wrong with Gladys?"

"Treacherous creature," she muttered.

All my happiness about Minerva whooshed away. "Why?" I whispered. "What has she done?"

Miss Frances shook her finger at Gladys. "She has thrown me—and not only me but also Miss Luther, who hurt her knee. She is gladsome for me no longer."

I stopped quite still and looked from Miss Frances to Gladys.

"Misfortune," Miss Frances said. "Misfortune and dread."

"Oh no," I said. "You're being too hard on Gladys."

"She is full of tricks and capers." Miss Frances's hot temper was in her voice. "I can't make her prance to suit me, so away she goes."

Poor Gladys. I went over and looked sadly down at her. "But you can't give up," I said. "You have the victory in you." I thought about the news I had to tell her. "And you give me courage."

Miss Frances just looked at me. She had given so many women courage. Maybe she was tired of doing that.

But I was almost as stubborn as she was. "What happened to having patience to begin again?" I asked. "What happened to up and out? Are you going to let a bicycle get the best of you?"

Miss Frances began to laugh. Finally, she caught her breath. "You are so good for me, Lillie," she said. "Perhaps the problem isn't a wobbling wheel at all, but a wobbling will."

———————✂———————

We spent the rest of the afternoon practicing with Gladys and talking. I told Miss Frances about the spelling bee, and she cried, "Bully for you!" She told me she was going to dig out her old woodworking tools and make me a boomerang. After supper, while we were walking Saint Courageous, she even quoted a bit of her speech for me. "When every woman shall say to every other, and every workman shall say to every other, 'Combine,' the war-dragon shall be slain, the poverty-viper shall be exterminated, the saloon drowned out, the last white slave liberated from the woods of Wisconsin and the streets of Chicago and Washington. For courage is as contagious as cowardice."

"I caught courage from you," I said.

"And I caught it from you." She raised one hand boldly to the sky. "Tell them the world was made for women, too!"

"Votes for women!" I shouted. We both laughed. Saint Courageous barked and barked.

Then I shook my head. "Do you think it will ever really happen, though? Most people aren't as strong as you are."

Miss Frances reached over and took my hand. "Almost everyone gives off some light in this world," she said gently. "But some people give off the light of a firefly. Others give off the light of a star. I believe that, as more of us choose to shine brightly, change will happen—a little at a time."

"Just like riding a bicycle," I said.

"Just like riding a bicycle." Miss Frances squeezed my hand tightly. "Even if it takes a long, long time and we fall often and bruise our knees."

I said good night and ran home grinning. Tiny stars, like sprinkles of salt, and also big, buttery ones were slathered on the dark sky. The smell of lilacs filled the air all around me. A person couldn't be around Miss Frances and still think of life as a web that trapped people like flies. A person could *do* things.

Yes, change was hard work and sometimes took a long, long time. I would miss Mother forever. Tomorrow, I would still have to look Hattie in the eye and probably listen to the hateful song again, and I would have to talk things out with Minerva. Maybe Father would say no to the bicycle. Maybe I'd have to think of a new plan. Miss Frances was in her fifties, and she had wanted to vote ever since she was a girl, but she still couldn't because of the law.

I knew Miss Frances would never give up, though. Neither would I. There had to be lots of good men out there, men like Father and Emery, who could change their minds. It might take a long time, but I was sure that someday Miss Frances and all the other women could do it. Maybe by the time Minerva and I were grown up, we would even be able to vote for the new president. Miss Frances and her speeches would keep us strong. After all, a woman who could ride a bicycle could do anything!

I ran up the steps to the front porch and turned around three times with my arms wide, as if I could hug the world. One thing I knew for sure. The last month—with all of the good and the bad—had certainly been the most marvelous, surprising, mind-changing, snake-waking month of my whole short life.

# Author's Note

For two years, I was director of downtown development for Trinidad, Colorado, a town that boomed in the late 1800s, when Coal was King. As I was doing research about people's lives during that time period, I ran across a few paragraphs about Frances Willard and how she learned to ride a bicycle. I was fascinated. In reading more, I discovered that this was a woman who traveled to every state and territory and gave speeches in thousands of towns. For ten years, she traveled fifteen to twenty thousand miles every year. Historians have called her the best-known woman of her time—and I had never heard of her.

I was also surprised to read that many experts thought the bicycle probably had more effect on women's rights than any other single thing. Finally, my research led to this work of historical fiction.

Frances Willard practiced riding Gladys throughout 1893, the year I chose for *Bicycle Madness*. For the purposes of the story, I moved her first bicycle ride from England to the Evanston, Illinois, neighborhood where she spent most of her life. Second, I changed her first ride from January to spring. Third, I gave her a fictional neighbor, a girl named Lillie.

Nearly every word Frances Willard speaks in this book is based on something she really did say or write. Some of the quotes that open chapters come from her books *Glimpses of Fifty Years* and *A Wheel Within a Wheel* and from an 1891 speech.

Except for Lillie's family and her teacher and classmates, the people in these pages are real (I did make up names for her pets), including the three men who appear in a photograph helping to support Gladys; Miss Luther, "an active minded young school teacher"; John Swinton, a New York newspaperman; Anna Gordon, Frances Willard's tireless secretary; Susan B. Anthony, who appeared before every U.S. Congress between 1869 and 1906 to speak on behalf of women's suffrage; and Florence Kelley, a Chicago reformer who proposed a bill creating a Factory Inspection Department and was appointed Chicago's first Chief Factory Inspector. "Webster's Blue-backed Speller," as it was often called, is also real. For many decades, U.S. schools relied on its moral lessons and vocabulary lists to help students learn to read and spell. In 1880, the publisher told an interviewer that his company was selling a million copies a year.

### WCTU: *The Fight for Temperance and Prohibition*

Frances Willard spent her life working for many things that are now an accepted part of U.S. society: child-labor laws, kindergartens for children, rights for workers. Her strongest opportunity to take a leadership position was as president of the Woman's Christian Temperance Union (WCTU), the largest women's organization in the United States in the late nineteenth century. She was its president from 1879 until she died.

Alcoholism was a major problem in the late 1800s, when women and children depended on men to earn the money that the family needed to live. The WCTU became a powerful voice for what was called "temperance" (choosing not to drink alcohol) and against the saloons that sold liquor. It was also one of the earliest opportunities for women to speak out politically about other issues. Frances Willard wrote that her work "tended more toward the liberation of women than . . . toward the extinction of the saloon."

### Votes for Women

In 1848, Elizabeth Cady Stanton and several other women organized a convention to be held in Seneca Falls, New York, where they announced their goal of gaining the right for women to vote. Three years later, Susan B. Anthony, a temperance advocate, became friends with Elizabeth Cady Stanton. These two strong women worked together for fifty years—and also had serious disagreements at times, some of which became public. For example, in 1881, Susan B. Anthony formed an alliance with Frances Willard and the WCTU and was publicly criticized for this action by Elizabeth Cady Stanton. In spite of their occasional "vexations" with each other, however, all three worked all their lives for women's right to vote.

The WCTU was multiracial—its membership included African-American women and Quaker women who had fought against slavery and also former slave owners. Frances Willard saw herself as a champion of African Americans, but Ida B. Wells, a young African-American woman who lived in Chicago and spoke out for women's rights and racial justice, called Frances Willard "no better or worse than the great bulk of white Americans" when it came to speaking out about racial injustices of the times. Their public conversation became heated as Ida B. Wells scolded Frances Willard for being too "timid" to speak out about violence toward African Americans and too worried about antagonizing the elite Southerners in the WCTU.

None of these four women was able to vote in her lifetime. Frances Willard died in 1898, twenty-two years before Congress passed the Nineteenth Amendment. But in the election of 1920, women the age Lillie would have been could finally go to the ballot box and drop in a vote for Warren Harding or James M. Cox for president of the United States.

### Prohibition

After many years of work by temperance reformers, the manufacture, sale, and transportation of alcohol became illegal with the Eighteenth Amendment to the U.S. Constitution in 1919. But such a thing was easier to declare than to enforce, and fourteen years later, in 1933, the Twenty-first Amendment to the U.S. Constitution repealed the Eighteenth Amendment.

### Bicycles

By the 1890s, women had been riding bicycles for a long time. The first women's bicycle race was held in 1868 on bicycles with huge front wheels (called "ordinaries"). In the 1880s, Queen Victoria had two tricycles, although no one knows whether she ever rode them. Frances Willard also owned a tricycle and broke her arm trying to better her own time in riding it around the block. But in the 1880s, the invention of the "safety" bicycle made cycling appealing to thousands of new riders, men and women.

Starting in 1889, there were lines of bicycles made just for women, the first one called a "Psycho Ladies Bicycle." Advertisements began to show ladies pedaling happily along. This trend alarmed many people, who lobbied for bicycle riding to be outlawed for girls and women and were outraged that female cyclists were taking up the wearing of "bloomers," a kind of loose trousers that had been around since the 1850s but never before really accepted. In New York, some men formed an Anti Bloomer Brigade, and in Chicago a woman was fined twenty-five dollars for wearing them. The bloomer fad faded by 1898, but by then women, for the most part, had given up their corsets as well as skirts down to their ankles.

The bicycle fad hit its peak around 1895–96, when there were about four million bicycle riders, including many women. Frances Willard was far from the first woman to pedal along on two wheels. As was true of so many things in her life, though, her example and her writings (in her book called *A Wheel Within a Wheel: How I Learned to Ride the Bicycle*) changed the minds of many respectable women. If a former dean of women and professor of English at Northwestern University and the current president of the WCTU could ride a bicycle—well!—who knew what brave things women could do next?

# Sources

Webster, Noah. *The American Spelling Book: Containing the Rudiments of the English Language, for the Use of Schools in the United States.* Bedford, Massachusetts: Applewood Books, 1999. (This book was originally published in 1824.)

Willard, Frances E. *Glimpses of Fifty Years: The Autobiography of an American Woman.* Chicago: Woman's Temperance Association Publication, 1889.

Willard, Frances E. *A Wheel Within a Wheel: How I Learned to Ride a Bicycle.* New York: Fleming H. Revell Company, 1895.